DIAMOND PARK DISCOVERY

Felix grabbed the bone and wiggled it. "It's loose," he said. He braced his feet on either side of the bone and pulled with all his might. His face turned red, and his arms shook with the strain.

Suddenly the bone came loose, and Felix went flying back into the mud.

Splat! He landed flat on his back.

Walter couldn't help laughing. Felix sat up, still holding on to the bone. He was covered in mud from head to foot.

"This is a tooth," he said slowly. "A tooth from a very, very large animal."

Walter glanced at the tooth. "Great. A tooth. That ought to round out your collection. Now can we go?"

Felix stood up and shook the bone at Walter. "Don't you get it! I think this is a dinosaur tooth!"

Other Bantam Skylark Books you will enjoy.
Ask your bookseller for the books you have
  missed.

THE CHOCOLATE TOUCH by Patrick Skene Catling

ENCYCLOPEDIA BROWN SOLVES THEM ALL
  by Donald J. Sobol

FELITA by Nicholasa Mohr

MAKE FOUR MILLION DOLLARS BY NEXT THURSDAY!
  by Stephen Manes

T. F. BENSON AND THE FUNNY-MONEY MYSTERY
  by David A. Adler

THE WHITE STALLION by Elizabeth Schub

THE NEVER SINK NINE

Diamond Park Dinosaur

BY GIBBS DAVIS

Illustrated by
George Ulrich

A SKYLARK BOOK
NEW YORK · TORONTO · LONDON · SYDNEY · AUCKLAND

For Bebe and Charles,
and their dinosaur-loving daughter,
Louisa

RL 2, 005-008

DIAMOND PARK DINOSAUR

A Skylark Book / May 1994

Skylark Books is a registered trademark of Bantam Books,
a division of Bantam Doubleday Dell Publishing Group, Inc.
Registered in U.S. Patent and Trademark Office and elsewhere.

ISBN 0-553-48131-2

Published simultaneously in the United States and Canada

Bantam Books are published by Bantam Books, a division of Bantam Doubleday Dell
Publishing Group, Inc. Its trademark, consisting of the words "Bantam Books" and the
portrayal of a rooster, is Registered in U.S. Patent and Trademark Office and in other
countries. Marca Registrada. Bantam Books, 1540 Broadway, New York, New York 10036.

PRINTED IN THE UNITED STATES OF AMERICA
O   0 9 8 7 6 5 4 3 2 1

CONTENTS

CHAPTER ONE

Rope Dope

Walter Dodd burst outside onto the empty playground at Eleanor Roosevelt Elementary School. Felix Smith had wandered off from gym class again, and Walter had volunteered to find him. Walter leaped over a rain puddle and stopped to cup his hands around his mouth.

"FEEEEELIX!"

Walter waited for an answer. He knew that by the time he found Felix, gym class would be over and he wouldn't have to try to climb the ropes. Felix never

1

had to participate in gym because of his asthma.

"Lucky duck." Walter sat down on a swing and tried to forget about gym class. He and Otis Hooper were the only ones who hadn't made it to the top of the ropes last year. Otis, Walter, and Felix were Never Sink Nine baseball teammates.

Walter slowly began swaying back and forth. *I'm a rope dope,* he thought. "Rope dope, rope dope, rope dope, rope dope, rope dope," he said, each time swinging a little higher. He watched his breath make clouds in the damp, chilly air.

"Ah-choo!"

Walter stopped swinging and turned around. The sneeze had come from the bushes behind him. "Felix, is that you?"

Walter was answered with another sneeze. He followed the sound and pushed back the bushes. A tall, skinny boy on his hands and knees was digging in the mud. "What are you doing, Felix?" he asked.

Felix Smith looked ridiculous. He was covered with mud. A magnifying glass hung from a string around his neck. Walter wished his best friend Mike Lasky were here so they could laugh at Felix together. It was harder to make fun of someone when you were alone.

Felix sat back on his knees and squinted at Walter through his glasses. "Hi, Walter. Got a Kleenex?"

"No," said Walter.

"That's okay." Felix wiped a muddy sleeve across his runny nose. It left a long brown streak across his face. "Don't you love mud season? It's the best time of year for rock hounds. You never know what'll turn up. My allergies are better, too."

Walter looked at Felix's runny red nose. It looked just the same as it did at

any other time of the year. "Mr. Keller wants you back in gym class," he said.

Felix started to get up.

Walter held out a hand to stop him. "There's no hurry." He glanced at his Babe Ruth wristwatch—four more minutes left of gym class. He tried to think of something to say to kill time. "Find any good rocks?"

Felix pushed back his Never Sink Nine cap and looked up at Walter. Felix was the worst player on their baseball team, but it never seemed to bother him. "I didn't know you liked rocks."

"Sure," said Walter, pretending to be interested.

"Look!" shouted Felix, pulling a small rock out of the mud. "A gastropod fossil!" He held up the ordinary-looking rock.

"A what?" Walter took the rock from Felix. There was a small spiral shape inside it.

"It's a snail fossil," Felix explained. "It's pretty common, but I'm going to add it to my collection of rocks, minerals, and fossils." He pulled out a pencil and small notebook and recorded his new find. Then he numbered the new specimen on a small label and put it in his pocket bulging with rocks.

Felix held up a pale yellow stone. "This one has pyrite in it. Watch." He struck it hard on another rock. Tiny sparks flew in all directions.

"Wow!" Walter stepped back. "How'd you do that?"

"It's got sulfur in it," said Felix. "I've got rocks that glow in the dark and ones that smell. It's fun. Want to help me with my collection?"

"Maybe," said Walter, checking his watch again.

"I could give you some of my rocks to start your own collection," said Felix.

"Yeah, I guess so," said Walter.

"Great!" Felix got up so quickly, some rocks fell out of his pockets. Walter helped him pick them up. Then Felix took Walter's hand and shook it until Walter's arm hurt. "It's official," said Felix, smiling hard. "We're rock hound partners. Tomorrow's Saturday. Want to come over and see my collection? We could go rock hunting afterward."

"Sure," said Walter. He heard the classroom bell ringing. Gym class was over. *Whew. I don't have to climb the ropes,* he thought, and started across the playground.

"Wait up!" Felix grabbed his rocks and tools and hurried after him, stopping to catch his breath once or twice.

By the time Walter and Felix got back to the gym, everyone had returned to their third-grade classrooms. A tall man in a sweatsuit was pulling mats out from under the ropes and piling them up in a corner. It was Mr. Keller, the gym teacher. "Give me a hand, boys," he said.

Walter and Felix helped stack the last mats. When they finished, Mr. Keller frowned at Felix and shook his head. "So where'd you run off to this time, Felix?"

Felix held out a handful of rocks. "Rock hunting." He blinked at the gym teacher from behind his glasses.

Mr. Keller didn't even look at the rocks. "Felix, you can't participate in gym because of your asthma," he said. "But you know you're supposed to stay and watch the rest of the class."

Felix stared down at the rocks in his hand.

"Next time, I'll have to report you to the principal," said Mr. Keller. "Understood?"

Felix nodded until his glasses slid down his nose. He looked scared.

Mr. Keller rested a hand on Walter's shoulder. "Because you went off rock hunting, Walter had to miss his turn at the ropes."

"Sorry, Walter," Felix said softly.

Walter couldn't look Felix in the eye. "That's okay," he said, turning away. He wanted to tell Felix that he had saved his life.

"I promise you'll be first in line to climb the ropes next time," added Mr. Keller.

Walter forced a smile. *Great,* he thought.

If it were up to Walter, they'd play baseball all year long. He swung an invisible bat through the air.

"Swooooooooooooosh!" he said.

"Miss baseball?" asked Mr. Keller.

"Yeah," said Walter.

"Don't you boys play at Diamond Park?" asked Mr. Keller, walking into the hall with them.

"Everyone does," said Walter. Felix nodded in agreement.

"You must be pretty upset with the news about Diamond Park then," said Mr. Keller.

"What news?" Walter was always interested in anything that had to do with baseball.

"Diamond Park's being turned into a shopping mall," Mr. Keller explained.

Walter felt as if he had been punched in the stomach. "*Our* Diamond Park?"

"When?" asked Felix.

"Any day now," said Mr. Keller. "They want to break ground while the earth's still soft. Mud season's the best time for that." Mr. Keller turned off down the hall and waved. "I'll see you two in class next week!"

Walter leaned against the wall and slid down to the floor.

"Are you okay, Walter?" asked Felix. "You don't look so hot."

CHAPTER TWO

No More Diamond Park

Walter and Felix were late getting back to their classrooms. They split up in the hall.

" 'Bye, Walt," said Felix, hurrying into Mr. Meyer's room. "Don't forget about rock hunting tomorrow."

"Rock hunting?" Walter was in a daze. His head was still spinning with the news about Diamond Park. "I've got to tell Mike," he said.

Walter burst into Mrs. Howard's

classroom. "Mike, something terrible has hap—" He stopped in midsentence. All of his classmates were in their seats staring at him.

"Welcome back, Walter," said Mrs. Howard in a stern voice. She looked at the clock on the wall. "Didn't gym class end almost fifteen minutes ago?"

Walter's ears burned. Everyone was waiting for his answer. "Mr. Keller asked me to find Felix!" he blurted.

Mike jumped up from his desk at the back of the room. "Walt's telling the truth. I was there!"

"Fine, Mike." Mrs. Howard grinned. "I believe you. Please take your seat, Walter. We're discussing our field trip to the Natural History Museum last week."

Walter hurried back to his seat next to Mike. "Thanks," he whispered.

Mike made an A-okay sign.

"Who else remembers some of the

things we saw at the museum?" asked Mrs. Howard.

No one raised a hand.

"How about the dinosaur fossils?" said Mrs. Howard. "Remember the life-size model of the Tyrannosaurus rex?"

Otis's hand shot up.

Walter wondered if Otis had made it to the top of the ropes in gym class today.

Mrs. Howard nodded in Otis's direction.

"The Tyrannosaurus rex is huge," Otis said. "He's over eighteen feet tall with eight-inch teeth. He's the largest meat-eating animal ever."

A dozen hands waved in the air. Mrs. Howard began calling on students one after another.

"Its head was twice as big as me," said Tony Pappas. He held up a picture he had just made of himself standing next to the dinosaur. Tony drew all the time and even had his own comic strip called *Sidelines* in the school newspaper.

Christy Chung stood up without waiting to be called on. She flung her long black hair over one shoulder. "My grandfather says the Chinese have been collecting dinosaur fossils for over two thousand years. Only they called them dragon bones." She sat down with a smug grin on her face.

"Very interesting, Christy," said Mrs. Howard. "Anyone else?"

The class was getting lively. But Walter couldn't think about anything but losing Diamond Park.

Mike raised his hand. "Dr. Mantell found the first dinosaur fossils," he said, proud that he had remembered.

Melissa Nichols, who had a long red ponytail and pony barrettes, looked back at Mike. "That's wrong," she said. "His wife, Mary Ann, found them. Her dumb husband just named them and took all the credit."

"No he didn't," said Mike, leaning forward over his desk.

"Yes he did," said Melissa, leaning back over her chair.

Mrs. Howard raised her hand as a warning. "That's enough about the Mantells. I think we can agree that together they found the first evidence of dinosaur fossils." She looked around the room. "Anyone else?"

A tall boy at the front of the class spoke up. "What do you call a dinosaur lollipop?"

Mrs. Howard smiled. "I give up, Pete. What?"

"A prehistor-lick."

Everyone laughed. Even Walter managed to forget about Diamond Park for a minute. He looked up at Pete Santos's Joke of the Day on the blackboard. It read:

Pete's Joke of the day Friday

What do you get when dinosaurs crash their cars?

Walter knew Pete had hidden the answer somewhere on the school grounds. He always did.

"Very good, class," said Mrs. Howard. "Now I'd like you all to get out paper and pencil and write one page on what impressed you most during our field trip."

Walter lifted the lid of his desk and reached inside for his notebook. His hand touched his leather baseball mitt. The news about Diamond Park came back to him. He looked at his Babe Ruth wristwatch. Half an hour until lunch. He didn't know if he could wait that long to tell Mike.

Walter took a deep breath and pulled out his notebook. He tried to think about dinosaurs. He started to write.

> The first dinosaur I ever saw was in a book. It said they all died 65 million years ago. That's a long time. I wonder if they played baseball back then?

Walter tried to think of something to add about the dinosaurs he'd seen at the museum.

> I was glad they didn't move.

17

Walter didn't want anyone to know he was afraid of something dead like dinosaurs. But he was. At the museum Walter thought he had seen the Tyrannosaurus rex move.

Walter looked at his last sentence. *It makes me sound like a scaredy cat,* he thought, and decided to erase it.

He lifted his desk top to find his eraser. It was in the shape of a little baseball. He rolled it in his hand. It wasn't white anymore. It was all dirty from erasing mistakes. *Taking away Diamond Park and putting in a shopping mall is a mistake, too,* he thought.

Walter felt as if he were going to explode if he didn't tell someone about Diamond Park that very minute. He looked across the aisle. Mike was pulling at his patchy hair. He was always getting baseball gum stuck in it and having Mrs. Howard cut it out.

"Pssssst." Walter made sure Mike was

looking and dropped his baseball eraser on the floor. Mike nodded. It was their secret signal to meet in the bathroom.

Walter raised his hand. "I have to go to the bathroom."

"Five minutes, Walter." Mrs. Howard didn't even look up from her desk.

Walter was already on his way out the door. He knew Mike would wait a minute and then ask to go to the bathroom, too.

Walter hurried to the boys' bathroom. He washed his hands to kill time until Mike showed up. Then he paced up and down the tiled floor. This was the worst thing that had ever happened to the Never Sink Nine since they'd started to play baseball together.

Walter remembered how the Never Sink Nine had begun. After being turned away from his older brother Danny's league and learning it was too late to join any other teams, Walter had taken

Grandpa Walt's advice and formed his own baseball team. *You just need nine,* Grandpa Walt had said.

Walter looked in the mirror at his baseball cap. He remembered the first time he put on his uniform with NEVER SINK NINE on the front and DODD 10 on the back. He'd felt like a real baseball player. He thought of the winning baseball he'd caught at their game against the Bulldogs. It was safely hidden inside his lucky socks at home.

Finally Mike burst into the bathroom.

"What's up?" he asked, stuffing a big pink square of bubble gum into his mouth. He only chewed the kind that came with baseball cards. "I think Mrs. Howard's suspicious. We'd better hurry."

Walter pointed to one of the bathroom stalls. "You better sit down."

"Sounds bad." Mike had just sat on a lowered toilet seat.

"It is," said Walter. He had just opened his mouth to tell Mike what he'd heard when the bathroom door was flung open.

It was Otis. "Hey, guys, what's going on?" He had a big, goofy smile on his face.

"This is a *private* meeting," said Mike. He chomped down hard on his gum.

Otis looked down at the tiled floor. "I had to go to the bathroom anyway," he whispered. But he didn't move.

"That's okay, Otis," said Walter. "I think you should hear this, too."

Otis's moonlike face broke into a smile again. Mike frowned and blew a giant bubble.

"Anyone who plays baseball should hear this," said Walter.

"That's practically the whole school," said Otis.

"That's practically every kid in Rockville," said Mike.

21

"Okay, here goes," said Walter, taking a deep breath. "Diamond Park is—"

Suddenly the bathroom door opened and banged back against the wall. This time it was Pete Santos. "What's going on?" Pete looked from Walter to Mike to Otis.

"It's about Diamond Park," said Otis.

"Something bad," said Mike. "Walter's the only one who knows."

"So what's the big deal?" said Pete. "I haven't got all day."

"They're going to tear up Diamond Park and put in a shopping mall!" Walter burst out. He had held in the news for so long, it was hard to hold back.

Otis, Mike, and Pete didn't say a word. They looked at Walter as if he had just thrown a bucket of ice-cold water on them.

Finally Pete blinked and managed to speak. "Is this a joke?"

"Of course not," said Mike. "Walter

wouldn't joke about something like this. Not Diamond Park!"

Everyone nodded solemnly.

"What're we going to do?" asked Otis. He looked as if he was about to cry. Mike offered him a piece of gum. Pete patted his back.

"People love to shop," said Pete. "My mom shops all the time."

"Mine does, too," said Mike. "Nothing can stop them from putting in a shopping mall."

"A dinosaur could," said Otis, his face turning red with anger. "A giant Tyrannosaurus rex with eight-inch teeth."

"A good magic trick could slow them down," said Pete. He was an amateur magician.

"Who're we kidding," said Mike. "Diamond Park is dead as dirt."

Pete shook his head. "I can't believe it. No more Diamond Park."

"No more Never Sink Nine," said Otis, blinking back tears.

Walter sighed. "No more baseball." He quickly bent down to tie his shoelaces. He didn't want his friends to see the tears welling up in his eyes.

Beneath the sink Walter spotted a slip of paper taped to the wall. The outside flap read *Pete's Joke of the Day—Friday —ANSWER*. Walter ripped it off the wall and stood up. "I found the answer to Pete's joke."

Any other time, Walter would have been thrilled. No one had ever found the answer to one of Pete's jokes before he told them where it was hidden.

"I don't remember what the joke was," Walter whispered.

" 'What do you get when dinosaurs crash their cars?' " said Pete.

Walter didn't have the heart to read the answer out loud. He lifted the flap and read the answer to himself. He passed the answer to Otis.

Otis read it out loud. " 'Tyrannosaurus *wrecks*.' That's a good one, Pete."

"Thanks," said Pete.

No one laughed. Diamond Park was about to die, and somehow it would have seemed disrespectful.

There was a knock on the bathroom door. "Boys, are you in there?" It was Mrs. Howard's voice.

Walter and Mike exchanged looks. "Uh-oh," they said together.

Mrs. Howard knocked again and opened the door a crack. "I'd like to speak to you in the hallway right now."

Pete was closest to the door, so he led the way. Otis, Mike, and Walter filed out behind him.

Mrs. Howard had her hands on her hips. There was a line down the middle of her forehead. She looked from Walter to Otis to Pete to Mike. "Can't I trust you boys to go to the bathroom for five minutes?"

"Sorry," mumbled Walter.

Everyone took Walter's lead and mumbled an apology, too.

Mrs. Howard sighed. "I can't imagine what was so important that it couldn't wait until lunch hour."

Walter heard Otis breathing fast beside him. Otis kept tightening his fists.

Suddenly Otis burst into tears. "They're getting rid of Diamond Park! They're turning it into a shopping mall!"

Walter swallowed hard to keep from crying, too. Mike was chewing his gum faster, and Pete was tugging hard on the tail of his shirt.

"It's not fair," said Mike.

Mrs. Howard's face softened. She put an arm around Otis and rubbed his back to comfort him. "I'm sorry, boys. I hadn't heard. I know how much Diamond Park means to you. But I'm sure there's someplace else in Rockville to play baseball."

Walter exchanged looks with his teammates. Mrs. Howard didn't understand. There was *no* place like Diamond Park.

At lunch hour in the cafeteria Walter rounded up the rest of the Never Sink Nine and told them the bad news.

"I guess that leaves more time for soccer," said Katie Kessler. "But I'll still miss playing baseball with you guys."

Melissa pulled her favorite toy horse, Misty, out of her backpack and hugged it tight. She started rocking back and forth. "We've never played baseball anywhere but Diamond Park."

Tony didn't say a word. Instead he kept his head bent over his sketchpad as he drew the Never Sink Nine baseball team standing on a sinking ship. Water was up to their waists, and sharks were swimming all around them.

Suddenly Christy Chung turned to Walter. "Your grandfather is our team's coach. He'll be able to help us. Won't he, Walter?"

Every Friday night, Walter's grandfather had dinner at the Dodds' house. *That's a great idea,* Walter thought. *Grandpa Walt will know exactly what to do.*

"I'll ask him for help tonight," Walter told his friends. Then he pointed to Tony's drawing and shook his head. "The Never Sink Nine hasn't sunk yet."

CHAPTER THREE

Shark Patrol

By the time school was out, it had stopped raining. Walter bicycled home as fast as he could. Sometimes Grandpa Walt arrived early on Friday to spend extra time with Walter and his brother Danny. Walter pedaled harder.

"Grandpa, Grandpa, Grandpa, Grandpa, Grandpa," Walter said, five times for good luck.

Walter turned up Elm Street and coasted into his driveway. He parked his bike and ran in the front door. "I'm hooooome!"

No one answered.

Walter headed for the kitchen to check for messages. He found the same old alphabet magnets and class photos of himself and Danny stuck on the refrigerator door. But no messages.

"Where is everybody?" said Walter, walking through the house. He thought he heard sounds coming from the basement. He stood at the top of the stairs and shouted, "MOM! Are you down there?"

Mrs. Dodd came slowly up the basement steps, wearing Mr. Dodd's old army boots and carrying a mop. "For goodness' sake, Walter, you don't have to shout."

"You look tired," said Walter.

"I am," she said, shoving the mop into Walter's hand. She kicked off the heavy army boots and sat down. "The basement flooded again. I've been down there all afternoon mopping. Can you finish the rest?"

"What about Danny?"

"He's delivering papers. He started his new job as a paperboy today. Remember?"

"He gets out of everything," said Walter. "It's not fair." He looked at his mother. Her hair was in a ponytail, but most of it had fallen down around her face. She looked so tired that Walter slipped his father's army boots on over his shoes without another word. "Mom, did you hear what they're doing to Diamond Park?"

"Tell me later, honey." Mrs. Dodd stood up and kissed him on the forehead. She gave him a little push toward the basement door. "I've got to get dinner started."

"But they're going to—"

"Later, Walter." Mrs. Dodd opened

the refrigerator door and began pulling out food. "I want the basement mopped before your father gets home. Sales have been slow at the car lot, and I don't want to upset him."

Walter dragged the mop behind him down the basement stairs. It seemed like no grown-up cared about Diamond Park.

Downstairs, one inch of water covered the concrete floor. Walter moaned just loud enough for his mother to hear him in the kitchen. Then he held out the mop like a sword ready to attack the enemy and crouched down on the last step.

"Charrrrge!" he said, and jumped into the water with a big splash.

By the time Walter had finished mopping, he was too tired to pull off his father's boots so he wore them to the dinner table. Mrs. Dodd looked at the boots but didn't say anything.

Walter counted the place settings. *One, two, three, four.* "Where's Grandpa Walt's place?" he asked.

"He can't make it tonight," replied Mrs. Dodd. She poured Walter a big glass of milk. "His bowling league has a tournament out of town."

"But I have to tell him about Diamond Park!" Walter wailed. Everything was going wrong. Grandpa Walt had been his only hope. *This is the end of the Never Sink Nine for sure,* he thought. What would he say to his friends now?

Just then, Mr. Dodd walked in and took his place at the head of the table. "What's wrong, Walt? You look like you just lost your best friend."

Walter rushed to his father's side. "They're turning it into a shopping mall, Dad!"

"Turning *what* into a mall?"

"Diamond Park." Walter's voice trembled.

Mr. Dodd put an arm around Walter and gave him a squeeze. "That's a shame, son. I know how you feel about the park. I learned to play ball there, too, when I was your age."

"Can't you stop 'em, Dad?" Walter asked.

"I don't think so, Walt." He looked thoughtful. "Isn't there a baseball field at the Y?"

"It's not the same," said Walter sadly. His father sounded like Mrs. Howard. Nobody understood.

Danny burst into the room. "I'm starved," he said, and reached across the table for a handful of rolls.

"So, Daniel, how does it feel to be a working man?" asked Mr. Dodd.

"Great," said Danny with a mouth full of bread. "I got through my whole route in less than two hours, and it was my first time."

Walter watched his older brother eat

the bread. Danny could help him, Walter decided. He played baseball, too. In fact, everyone called him Danny the Driver, king of the home runs. He wouldn't take this sitting down.

"They're getting rid of Diamond Park!" Walter said, interrupting Danny's conversation with their father.

Danny looked at Walter. "That's old news," he said. "It was in yesterday's paper. Front page, second section."

"What should we do?" asked Walter.

"Nothing," Danny answered. "You can always find another place to play ball. Besides, I'm not going to have time for that kid stuff with my new job. You heard Dad—I'm a working man now."

Danny and Mr. Dodd smiled at each other. Walter looked down. Didn't anyone care about Diamond Park?

"You'll feel better after you eat something, Walter," said Mrs. Dodd. She set a platter of chicken in front of him. "Help yourself."

Walter took a bite of chicken leg. He still felt just as bad.

"The basement flooded again, and Walter did a super job of helping mop up," announced Mrs. Dodd.

"Good work, Walt," said Mr. Dodd.

Walter sat up straight and smiled back at his father. "I'm a working man, too. Right, Dad?"

"Certainly," said Mr. Dodd.

"Turkey brain," whispered Danny. But Walter ignored it.

"I almost forgot," said Mrs. Dodd. "Felix Smith called while you were in the basement, Walter. He said not to forget about coming over tomorrow and to bring your boots."

Walter groaned. He had forgotten his promise to go rock hunting with Felix.

"Isn't Felix the skinny kid with the runny nose?" said Danny.

"He doesn't have a runny nose," said Walter. "He's got allergies."

"Boogers are boogers," said Danny.

"That's enough, boys," said Mrs. Dodd. "Let's eat the rest of our meal in peace. Then *both* my working boys can wash and dry tonight's dishes."

Walter and Danny moaned together.

Later that night, Walter decided to wear his Never Sink Nine uniform to bed for old times' sake. He went into the bathroom to look at himself in the full-length mirror.

" 'Bye, Diamond Park," Walter said to his reflection. He took a deep breath and watched the little plunger on his chest expand one last time. " 'Bye, Never Sink Nine."

Walter hung his head and closed his eyes the way he saw people do in the movies when someone died. In one day he had lost Diamond Park, failed to climb the ropes at school, and had to mop up the basement.

Walter opened his sock drawer and took out the lucky socks Grandpa Walt had given him after their first game.

"Perfect," said Walter, breathing in the stinky socks. They had never been washed in order to keep their luck. Inside one of the socks was his treasured baseball.

Walter carried it over the line of tape that divided his and Danny's bedroom and crawled into bed. He placed the ball and socks under his pillow. He thought about his mitt sitting all alone in the dark inside his desk at school. "Diamond Park's all alone in the dark, too," he whispered. He thought about the Babe Ruth diamond, the Willie Mays diamond, and the Mickey Mantle diamond and how they wouldn't be there this summer as they always had been.

Walter wanted to cry, but he was too tired. Missing things was exhausting. He stretched out and looked up at the solar system mobile he had made with Grandpa Walt. He watched the planets slowly spin around the sun until he drifted to sleep. Then he began to dream.

Nine dinosaurs appeared on a huge ship with NEVER SINK painted on its side. Eight of them were playing a game of catch. The other dinosaur wore socks, and he was mopping the deck and watching the water pour onto the sinking ship.

"We're sinking!" cried the dinosaur in socks.

"Don't be prehistoric," said a dinosaur wearing glasses. "We're on the *Never Sink* ship. How could we sink?"

The water was rising quickly. The dinosaur in socks mopped faster and faster. Suddenly sharks appeared and began circling the ship.

"Help!" cried Walter. "Sharks! Sharks!"

Danny was holding on to his shoulders and shaking him. "Wake up, Walter. It's a nightmare."

Walter sat up wide-eyed in bed. He blinked at his brother and took a quick look around the room. No sharks. No dinosaurs.

"Want some water?" Danny offered him his squirt gun.

Walter thought of the sinking ship. "No!" he said loudly. "No water!"

"Okay, okay," said Danny. "Why are you acting so weird?"

Walter looked down at the sheets twisted around his legs. "Diamond Park," he whispered, expecting Danny to make fun and call him a turkey brain. But Danny didn't say one word. Walter looked over at his brother sitting on the edge of his bed. Danny's face was scrunched up as if he was going to cry.

"You know, you're not the only one who feels crummy about Diamond Park," said Danny. Suddenly he got up and turned out the light.

Walter pulled up his sheets and settled back against his pillow. He felt better just knowing Danny felt crummy about Diamond Park, too.

He tried to see his brother's twin bed in the dark. "You were on my side of the room," said Walter.

"Shut up, turkey brain," said Danny with a laugh. "Go to sleep, or I'll call the shark patrol."

Walter smiled. Some things never changed.

CHAPTER FOUR

Inch by Inch

Walter was coming downstairs for breakfast when he heard a knock on the front door. "I'll bet it's Grandpa Walt!" He jumped the last two steps and flung the door open.

"Hi, Grand—" Walter stopped in midsentence and stared at the boy on his doorstep. It was Felix Smith.

"Hi, Walt." Felix wiped his nose on his jacket sleeve and smiled. "You've never been to my house before. Thought

44

you might need some help getting there."

Walter looked at his Babe Ruth wristwatch. "It's seven in the morning, Felix. I haven't even eaten breakfast yet." He waited for Felix to turn and go.

Felix shrugged. Two small rocks fell out of a pocket. "That's okay. I can wait. Rock hounds are good at waiting. It takes a long time to find the perfect specimen."

"Forget it," said Walter. "Let's just go. I'm not that hungry." *The sooner I get this over with, the more time I'll have to hang out with Mike later,* he thought.

Walter grabbed his boots on the way out. " 'Bye, Mom!" he shouted. "I'm going rock hunting with Felix!" His father was already at the car lot, and Danny was asleep upstairs.

Walter rolled his bike out of the garage. Felix just stood in the driveway, blinking at Walter behind his glasses. "I don't have all day," said Walter. "Get your bike, and let's go."

"I don't have a bike," said Felix.

Walter stared at Felix as if he were an alien from outer space. "What do you mean, you don't have a bike. How do you get around?"

"I walk," said Felix. "You never know when you'll find something along the road."

Walter hit his hand against his forehead. "I don't believe this." He straddled his bike. "Hop on," he said, nodding back toward the bike seat. "We're not walking."

Felix sat on the seat behind Walter.

Walter pushed off. "Where to?" he asked.

"My house first," Felix said. "I'll show you my collection. Then we can pick up my equipment and go rock hunting."

"Fine," Walter said, already irritated.

On the way to Felix's house, Felix pointed out the different kinds of rock in everything they passed. "There's granite in that building, and the roof is slate," he said. "The glass is pure sandstone."

By the time they reached Felix's house, Walter was fed up with rocks *and* Felix. He parked the bike in front of the house and faced Felix. "Why do you collect rocks, anyway?" he demanded. "It's weird."

Felix looked hurt. "I don't know. People collect all kinds of things. Mike collects baseball cards."

Walter thought about all the bus equipment that Grandpa Walt had collected in his apartment. Some people thought the steering wheel mounted over his mantel was weird, too, but Grandpa Walt loved it. It reminded him of the bus he had driven for twenty-eight years.

"The oldest things you can collect are rocks," said Felix. "Most of them are millions of years old. Rocks cover the whole earth. No matter where you live, you live on rock."

"Really?" said Walter. He hadn't known that.

Felix looked away from Walter. "Sorry I made you miss your turn at the ropes in gym yesterday."

Walter dug his hands deep in his pockets. Somehow he couldn't keep his secret any longer.

"I hate the ropes," Walter confessed. "I wanted to find you so I'd miss my turn. I can't climb. I'll never make it to the top."

Felix didn't say anything. He just stood there rubbing two rocks together.

He thinks I'm a rope dope, thought

Walter. *He'll tell everyone, and I'll have to run away.*

Felix put the rocks back into his pocket. "You can make it. I've watched you in gym. You just need to use your feet and legs more. That's your problem."

"Huh?" Walter couldn't believe Felix had paid that much attention. "How come you know so much about climbing? You've never even been on the ropes."

Felix shrugged. "I watch. All the good climbers grip with their feet and push themselves up." He walked over to a tire swing that was hanging from a rope on a tree next door to his house. "Try it," he said. "My neighbors won't mind."

Walter shook his head. "I can't."

"That's okay," said Felix. "I'll show you some other time. Inch by inch, anything's a cinch. You'll see."

Walter followed Felix into the house.

An elderly woman was sitting in the living room watching TV.

"Hi, Mrs. Thomas," said Felix, walking back into the kitchen. "Mom works Saturdays, so it's just me and Mrs. Thomas," he explained. "Hungry?"

"Starved," said Walter, sitting down at the kitchen table. He hoped Mrs. Thomas knew how to make waffles like his mother.

"How about a sedimentary sandwich?"

"What's that?"

"You'll see." Felix got out a loaf of bread, a jar of peanut butter, and a jar of grape jelly. He began making a peanut butter and jelly sandwich.

"That's just a P and J," said Walter. He didn't really mind because it was crunchy peanut butter, his favorite.

"A sedimentary rock is built up in layers like this," said Felix. He spread a layer of jelly on top of a layer of crunchy peanut butter. "After years and years the layers stick together." He laid a piece of bread on top and pressed down. The layers of peanut butter and jelly squished out the sides.

Walter licked his lips.

Felix lifted a salt shaker from the table. "Salt is made from rock, too. Rock salt."

"Cool," said Walter. "What else is made of rock?"

"My glasses," said Felix, pushing his heavy glasses back up his nose. "And my mom's face powder. Talc is the softest mineral, and rocks are made of minerals." He handed Walter his sandwich and then led him down a hall to his bedroom. "Here it is," he said, opening the door. "Rock central."

Walter couldn't believe his eyes. The walls were covered with geology charts and big, colorful posters of dinosaurs. The floor was a minefield of cardboard boxes and bags filled with specimens.

"Watch your step." Felix made his way across the room, stepping between the piles.

Walter opened an egg carton filled with small rocks that glowed. Beside the carton was a matchbox filled with the tiniest bits of rock. Taped to the door was a photo of an old man. "Who's he?" asked Walter. "Your grandfather?"

"That's Goethe," said Felix. "He was a famous poet. But he collected minerals, too. They named a mineral after him. Goethite. I want a rock named after me someday."

Walter carefully stepped over rock piles and scattered field notes to the bed. He sat down to eat his sandwich. "I know what you mean. I want a baseball field named after me." Walter had never told that to anyone before. Not even Mike.

"The Walter Dodd field," Felix an-

nounced over a pretend loudspeaker. "Sounds good."

"Walter *P.* Dodd," corrected Walter.

"Even better," Felix agreed. "More important-sounding."

Felix showed Walter his collection of minerals. He struck one called mispickel with a rock and held it under Walter's nose.

"It smells like garlic," said Walter.

"Watch this," said Felix. He held some paper clips near a mineral called magnetite. The paper clips were pulled to it as if it were a magnet.

"Look through this one." Felix held a clear piece of calcite over a book. All the letters appeared double.

"Pete could use these minerals in his magic act," said Walter. He never knew rocks and minerals could be so much fun.

"It takes millions of years for some

rocks to form," said Felix. "They're really strong."

Walter watched Felix as he sorted through his cabinets of drawers filled with rocks, minerals, and fossils. He tried on Felix's rock-hunting goggles and looked at himself in the mirror. He looked as goofy as Felix did, but it was fun.

Felix is strong like his rocks, Walter realized. *He has to be strong to be so different from everyone else at school.*

Felix got out his new dinosaur book. They looked at the triceratops with a three-horned face and a brachiosaurus as tall as a four-story building. " 'The supersaurus and ultrasaurus weigh as much as twenty elephants,' " Felix read.

Walter looked at the stegosaurus. "It says they have brains the size of a walnut. That must be why they were so dumb and died out."

Felix shook his head. His glasses slipped down his nose and he pushed them back up again. "Just because they had small brains doesn't mean they were stupid. They lived for almost a hundred and forty million years. No dummies live that long. That's seventy-five times longer than people have lived."

I've only lived eight and three-quarters years, thought Walter.

Felix pulled something out of a drawer marked *Fossils* and handed it to Walter. It was a big, shiny, pointed tooth surrounded by rock.

"What is it?" Walter touched the sharp point.

"A shark tooth," said Felix. "A very, very old shark tooth."

Walter drew back his hand as if the tooth might bite. He remembered his dream of the sinking ship surrounded by sharks. Suddenly he wanted to get out of

Felix's room filled with old bones and shark teeth. "Let's go," he said.

Felix grabbed his rock-hunting gear, and they were out the door.

Walter pushed off with Felix behind him on the bicycle seat. "Where to now?" he asked.

"Diamond Park," said Felix. "The plows are already ripping up the Babe Ruth diamond. We might find some good stuff in all that churned-up mud."

As Walter slowly pedaled toward Diamond Park, he felt as if someone had thrown a hundred-mile-an-hour fastball into his chest.

CHAPTER FIVE

Treasure in the Mud

"See where they started plowing?" Felix pointed across Diamond Park to a big yellow steam shovel. "I found my first fossil there last year. Let's go take a look."

Walter followed in Felix's muddy footprints until he caught sight of his beloved Babe Ruth diamond. Most of it had already been plowed over. The baseball diamond had been torn up, and the pitcher's mound was flattened.

"No!" Walter's heart beat faster as

he ran through ankle-high mud to where his position at second base had been. It was gone, buried under the mud. The steam shovel was parked right on top of it.

Walter gave the machine a kick. "That's *my* position you're on!" He sank against the steam shovel and sighed.

A cold wind blew across Diamond Park. Walter jammed his hands into his pockets. All he could think about was baseball and the way Diamond Park used to be. Felix was down on his hands and knees digging for rocks where home plate had been last year.

I can't believe I'm here hunting rocks instead of batting balls, Walter thought. He swung an imaginary bat through the air.

"Swooooosh!" he said.

He hit an imaginary ball. "Crack!"

Walter threw down the pretend bat and ran the bases. The mud pulled at his boots. But he kept running until he crossed home plate, where he nearly ran into Felix.

Walter cupped his hands around his mouth like a loudspeaker. "Dodd hits a home run, and the crowd goes wild!" He made a muffled sound like the cheering of a crowd.

Felix was pulling at something in the mud. He stopped to watch Walter. "Remember Never Sink's first game last season?"

"Sure," said Walter. "We played the Bulldogs."

"You caught the winning ball in the last inning," said Felix.

Walter smiled until his face hurt. He hadn't thought Felix would remember.

"Give me a hand," said Felix. He was digging around a long white thing sticking up out of the earth. "I think I found a bone or something."

"I don't feel like rock hunting," said Walter. "Let's go home."

Felix handed Walter a small chisel. "Come on, Walter. Give me a hand. We'll leave right after I dig this out. Okay?"

"It's just a big dog bone," said Walter. But he took the chisel and started picking at the hardened dirt surrounding the bone. He knew it was no use trying to talk Felix out of it.

Felix grabbed the bone and wiggled it. "It's loose," he said, breathing hard with excitement. He braced his feet on either side of the bone and pulled with all his might. His face turned red, and his arms shook with the strain.

Suddenly the bone came loose, and Felix went flying back into the mud.

Splat! He landed flat on his back.

Walter couldn't help laughing. Felix sat up, still holding on to the bone. He was covered in mud from head to foot.

"Let's go," said Walter, turning to leave.

Felix didn't move. He pulled a rag

out of his pocket and wiped off his new specimen. It was eight inches of shiny white bone with a pointed tip. Even though it was caked with mud, the point was razor-sharp. As Felix turned the bone over and over in his hands, he began sneezing.

"Ah-choo! Aaaaaah-choo! *Ah-choooo!*"

Walter looked around the park for someone to help. "Are you having an allergy attack or something?"

Felix shook his head and tried to calm down. He stared at the bone as if he couldn't believe what he was seeing. "This is a tooth," he said slowly. "A tooth from a very, very large animal."

Walter glanced at the tooth. "Great. A tooth. That ought to round out your collection. Now can we go?"

Felix stood up and shook the bone at Walter. "Don't you get it! I think this is a dinosaur tooth!"

• • •

After Felix cleaned himself off with a rag, Walter bicycled Felix and the giant tooth to the same Natural History Museum that they had visited on their class field trip.

When the boys got into the museum, a friendly security guard helped them find Dr. Wilson, a museum geologist and dinosaur expert.

When Dr. Wilson saw the huge tooth, he agreed to take a look at it in his workshop. He studied the tooth under a magnifying glass and then under a big microscope while Walter and Felix sat quietly among shelves of bones and skeletons.

Walter jabbed Felix. "This place gives me the creeps," he whispered.

"It'd be great on Halloween," said Felix.

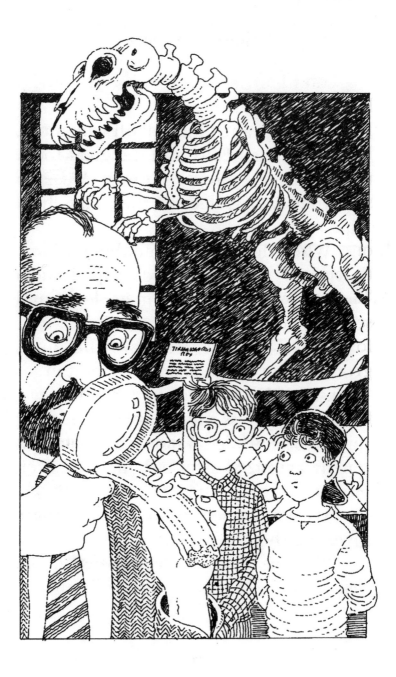

After half an hour, Dr. Wilson finally looked up. "This could be big news for Rockville, boys. I mean *really* big." Then he opened a large book and started flipping through the pages. "Hmmmm," he said, rubbing his chin thoughtfully.

Walter couldn't stand the suspense one second longer. He got up and tapped Dr. Wilson on the shoulder. "Could we enter this tooth in the school science fair?" Walter was always looking for ways to get extra credit since his grades weren't that hot.

A smile broke out on Dr. Wilson's face. "Son, this *is* the science fair."

"What is it?" asked Felix. He was about to sneeze.

"You've just dug up the first Tyrannosaurus rex fossil ever found in this part of the country."

"Ah-choo! Ahh-choo! Ah-choo! Ah-choo!" Felix didn't stop sneezing for ten minutes.

CHAPTER SIX

Dinosaur Park

"I don't look any more famous," said Walter, peering at himself in the bathroom mirror. It had been a whole week since he and Felix had found the dinosaur tooth. Since then, they had become famous at school and around town. Everyone was talking about the rare fossil and how amazing it was that two third-graders had been the ones who discovered it. Being famous was almost enough to make Walter forget about what was happening at Diamond Park.

Danny banged on the bathroom door. "Did you die in there? Open up!"

"Go away!" said Walter. "I'm rehearsing my lines."

Today Mr. Dodd had asked Walter and his Never Sink Nine teammates to do a special television commercial for his car lot. Because everyone in town was so excited about the dinosaur fossil, Mr. Dodd had decided to have a sale and call it Dodd's Dinosaur Days.

"I've got something for you," said Danny.

Walter opened the door. Danny stood there holding a rolled-up newspaper. "Wish I didn't have to miss your commercial," Danny said. "But I've got my newspaper route."

"Don't worry," said Walter. "If you're lucky, I'll tell you about it at dinner tonight."

Danny gave Walter a bop on the head with his newspaper.

"Hey, watch it," said Walter. "You squashed my dinosaur hat." His father had given him a cap with a little stuffed dinosaur driving a car on top.

"That's to keep you from getting a big head, turkey brain," said Danny. "Besides, Rockville's gone dinosaur crazy, if you ask me. Look!" He unrolled the newspaper and shoved it in front of Walter.

Walter read the headline:

ROCK HOUND ROCKS ROCKVILLE
LOCAL BOYS PUT TOWN ON MAP

Below the headline was a map of the United States with an arrow pointing to the small town of Rockville. Beside the map was a photo of Dr. Wilson with his arms around Felix and Walter. Felix was holding the dinosaur tooth.

"Thanks," said Walter, tearing off the page and folding it carefully into his pocket. "I'll put it in my scrapbook with the other articles." He still couldn't believe it. Walter had gotten more attention in one week than he'd gotten in his whole life.

Suddenly he heard someone honking from the driveway.

"It's Grandpa Walt," said Walter, heading for the stairs. He waved back to Danny. "See you at dinner!"

Grandpa Walt was waiting in his station wagon. "Ready to pick up the rest of the team?" he said, pulling out of the driveway.

"Yeah," said Walter. He noticed Grandpa Walt was wearing his Coach sweatshirt and Never Sink Nine team cap. "It feels funny picking up everyone when we're not playing baseball today."

Grandpa Walt smiled and nodded. "I know what you mean, champ."

By the time they reached Mr. Dodd's car lot, the television director and his crew had already set up the lights and cameras. Mrs. Dodd was serving soda in dinosaur cups to all the customers.

"Thanks for doing this commercial for me, kids," said Mr. Dodd. "You all look great in your dinosaur hats and T-shirts."

The director placed Walter and the Never Sink Nine team in front of a row of cars. Walter stood between Felix and a six-foot inflatable dinosaur. A banner hung above his head that read DODD'S DINOSAUR DAYS/ROCK BOTTOM PRICES.

"Ready, camera, action!" said the director. He pointed to Felix.

Felix pushed up his glasses and squinted into the television camera. "Don't miss Dodd's Dinosaur Days. Get prehistoric prices on good-as-new used cars."

Mike and Melissa pointed to a map of downtown Rockville they were holding between them. "You can't miss it," they said together. "On the corner of Third and Jefferson in beautiful downtown Rockville."

The director pointed to Walter.

Walter took a deep breath and recited his lines. "I'm Walter P. Dodd, and I ought to know."

Then the rest of the team chimed in with Walter. "Stop driving those old Tyrannosaurus wrecks, and come in to Dodd's today!"

The director gestured for everyone to smile and wave.

Walter flashed a big smile and waved good-bye into the camera with both hands.

"Cut!" said the director. "Beautiful. Print it. Good work, kids."

"Anyone want to go to the Pizza Palace?" Grandpa Walt was twirling his car keys around on one finger.

"Yes!" shouted Walter and his friends. Everyone piled into the station wagon.

Walter slid into the front seat next to Grandpa Walt. He tugged on Grandpa Walt's sleeve and whispered in his ear, "But we always went to the Pizza Palace after a baseball game."

"You don't have to play baseball to have fun with your friends," Grandpa Walt told him softly.

"Or eat pizza," said Mike, sliding in next to Walter.

"Games come and go," added Grandpa Walt. "Even dinosaurs disappear. But as long as people are around, friends will stick together."

When they got to the Pizza Palace, everyone talked about where they were going to play baseball from now on.

"Walt and I will work on finding a new field by baseball season," said

Grandpa Walt. "Don't worry. The Never Sink Nine is alive and well."

Felix stood up and tapped a spoon against his glass to get everyone's attention. "Mayor Higsby wants Walt and me to come up with a new name for Diamond Park, and we want you to help because that's where we started playing baseball together and got to be a team."

Walter knew it was his turn to talk when Felix looked at him. "Write a new name for Diamond Park on your paper napkin and give it to me," he said. "Then come to the renaming ceremony next Saturday at Diamond Park."

Everyone took a long time writing down their choice. Otis erased his paper napkin so many times, it shredded and he had to get a new one.

Walter stared at his napkin, just thinking. So much had happened this week that he had almost forgotten about Diamond Park. He had always dreamed that he'd become a famous baseball player on the field. It was funny to think that what had made him and Felix famous instead was an old dinosaur bone.

Walter glanced at Grandpa Walt, and the older man gave him a wink. *It will be okay*, Walter thought. *Grandpa Walt will help us find a new field, and the Never Sink Nine will be together again this spring.*

Suddenly Walter had an idea. He knew what his new name for Diamond Park would be. Quickly he straightened out his napkin and wrote down his choice.

The following Saturday, Walter rode his bicycle to Diamond Park with Mike. When they got to the park, the entire Babe Ruth field was covered with Rockville folks. There was a big tent over the site where the Tyrannosaurus rex was being dug up. Next to the dig site was a wooden platform where Mayor Higsby and Dr. Wilson were standing next to a big easel covered by a sheet.

"I'm your best friend," Mike said to Walter as they parked their bikes. "Tell me what you named the park."

"Can't," said Walter. "I told you. I promised not to." Walter wanted to tell Mike more than anything. He was glad he didn't have to keep the secret much longer.

Walter spotted Felix's blue and white Never Sink Nine cap in the crowd. "There's Felix!" he said, pushing past the people. Felix was surrounded by reporters asking him questions. Newscasters held out microphones and cameras flashed.

Melissa waved to Walter and Mike

and joined them. "Wow, I never thought our team would be famous because of some dinosaur bones," she said.

"Yeah," said Mike. "We're kind of celebrities, too."

Mayor Higsby raised his hand for everyone to stop talking. It was time for the ceremony to begin. Walter and Felix scrambled onstage.

Walter looked at Felix standing next to him on the platform. He was still the same goofy-looking kid with pockets bulging with rocks. But something was different. No one was laughing at Felix today.

"Welcome to the renaming of Diamond Park!" Mayor Higsby boomed over the loudspeaker. Everyone clapped. Mayor Higsby raised a hand, and the crowd quieted down again. "As you know, a record-breaking fossil of a Tyrannosaurus rex has been found by our own Felix Smith and Walter Dodd. Diamond Park has been proclaimed an official archaeological dig site. Dr. Wilson tells me that digging up dinosaurs is not an easy job, but anyone who wishes to help may sign up after this ceremony. Now I'd like to present Dr. Wilson, world-renown geologist and expert on dinosaur fossils."

Dr. Wilson took the microphone. "Welcome, Rockvillians! Today is a momentous occasion. The Tyrannosaurus rex, king of the tyrant lizards, has been found in your own back yard. Our guest of honor today is Felix Smith, the eight-year-old boy who led us to this dinosaur skeleton—"

"And Walter Dodd, too!" yelled the Never Sink Nine.

"Indeed yes." Dr. Wilson acknowledged Walter with a smile before continuing. "When scientists make such discoveries, they usually give each dinosaur a name. It has been decided that Felix will name your Rockville dinosaur because he first sighted the fossil. Felix?"

Everyone clapped and cheered as Felix took the microphone. He blinked into the flashing lights as news photographers snapped his picture.

Felix cleared his throat. "I've decided to name the dinosaur Felix. First of all because I found him, and second of all because *Felix* means 'good fortune.' I'd also like to say something to my fellow rock hounds. Keep looking, because you never know when you'll find something." Felix handed the microphone to Walter.

"And now for the renaming of Diamond Park," announced Walter. "My teammates and I love Diamond Park because we love baseball. But the dinosaurs were here first, and fair's fair." The Never Sink Nine filed onstage. Walter signaled to Mike. A drum roll began as Otis, Melissa, and Mike pulled the sheet off the easel. Walter and the rest of Rockville read the plaque underneath:

Mike looked at Walter and grinned. *He likes the name,* Walter thought. He smiled back at his friend as everyone clapped. The ceremony was over.

"Let's go sign up to help dig out the dinosaur bones," said Pete. Melissa followed behind Pete.

"Are you going to sign up?" Otis asked Walter.

"Nah," said Walter. "Who wants to dig up a bunch of old bones when baseball season's coming up?"

Otis leaned over and whispered in Walter's ear, "We have the ropes again on Monday. I'm staying home and pretending to be sick."

"We can't run away from those ropes forever," said Walter.

They heard Felix's voice behind them. "The ropes are right here. Why don't you both get some practice?"

Otis and Walter looked at each other.

"Come on." Felix led the way to the playground on the edge of the park. Walter and Otis followed behind without saying a word. They stopped beneath two climbing ropes that hung above a sandbox.

"I'll go first," said Walter, feeling braver than usual.

"No," said Otis. "Let's try it together." He wiped his hands on his jeans and grabbed the other rope. "Now what?"

"Start climbing," said Felix.

Walter's arms trembled as he tried to pull himself up. His feet slid down the rope.

Felix grabbed hold of his feet and arranged them so they wound around the rope. "Now push up with your feet," he said. "Don't forget to use your legs."

Walter moved up a few inches.

"Grip the rope with your feet again," said Felix.

Walter took a deep breath and did as he was told. He inched up the rope little by little, stopping to rest each time. Finally he was so close to the top, he could reach out and touch it. "I did it!" he shouted. He looked across at Otis. Felix was urging him on. "Come on, Otis. You can do it!" said Walter.

Otis gritted his teeth and pulled

himself up high enough to touch the top. "I did it, too!" An enormous smile of relief and joy spread over his face.

Felix gave them both a thumbs-up sign.

It was much faster sliding down the rope. Walter and Otis gave each other high-fives. They couldn't stop smiling as they started home.

"You were right, Felix," said Walter. "Inch by inch, anything *is* a cinch."

CHAPTER SEVEN

R. I. P.

Monday after school, Walter and some of his Never Sink Nine friends burst out of Eleanor Roosevelt Elementary. As they headed for the bike rack, Tony held up his drawing pad. It was his newest SIDELINES comic strip.

Everyone smiled. "That's funny," said Mike.

When they reached the bikes Melissa shifted her bag of toy horses onto her back and climbed onto her bike. "Race you to Dinosaur Park."

"I can come, too," said Mike. "I don't have piano lessons today." He pulled a hammer and pick just like Felix's out of his backpack. Almost every kid in Rockville had rock-hunting equipment now.

"Aren't you going to help dig?" Otis shouted after Walter.

"Later!" Walter shouted back. "I'll meet you there. I have something to do first!"

Walter took the long route home.

Today had been so wonderful, he never wanted it to end. In gym class he and Otis had climbed all the way to the top of the ropes.

He coasted into downtown Rockville past his father's car lot. Business was booming. "Hi, Dad!" Walter shouted.

Mr. Dodd looked up from a customer and waved. He was wearing a hat with a tiny stuffed dinosaur on top.

A bus loaded with tourists wearing dinosaur T-shirts was parked in front of Klugman's Drugstore on Main Street. Walter stopped in for a cherry Popsicle. On his way out, a stranger stopped him on the street for directions.

"Which way is the dinosaur?" asked the young man.

Walter pointed and gave him directions. He felt important.

As soon as Walter got home, he went straight up to his bedroom. He opened the sock drawer and pulled out his lucky socks. One of the socks had a big bulge in the heel. Walter reached in and pulled out the old dirty baseball. Some of the red stitching had come undone. It was the winning ball he had caught at the Never Sink Nine's first game on the Babe Ruth diamond last season.

Walter picked up one of his mother's gardening shovels on his way outside. He circled the back yard a few times until he found the perfect spot.

"This is it," he said, plunging the shovel into the ground to dig the hole. He dug it just deep enough and wide enough.

Walter took the baseball out of his pocket and rolled it in his hands. Then he laid it gently in the hole and buried it. "Someday millions of years from now, when baseball is forgotten like the dinosaurs, someone will find you," said Walter. "And baseball will be remembered and begin all over again."

DIAMOND PARK DINOSAUR

This must have been how Tyrannosaurus rex felt before he became extinct, Walter thought. Everything was changing all around him, too—the Babe Ruth diamond, even Rockville. Walter was glad that if Diamond Park had to be renamed, it was for the dinosaurs. At least people were remembering them.

"Dinosaurs had small brains, but I'll bet they had big hearts," said Walter. "I wouldn't be afraid of them anymore."

Walter's mother leaned out the kitchen window. "What are you doing in my garden, Walter!"

"Nothing," said Walter. He got back on his bike and headed for Dinosaur Park. He had the whole rest of the afternoon to spend with his friends.

ABOUT THE AUTHOR

GIBBS DAVIS was born in Milwaukee, Wisconsin, and graduated from the University of California at Berkeley. *Walter's Lucky Socks, Major-League Melissa, Slugger Mike, Pete the Magnificent, Tony's Double Play, Christy's Magic Glove, Olympic Otis,* and *Katie Kicks Off* are all part of the Never Sink Nine series for First Skylark. Gibbs divides her time between New York City and Wisconsin.

ABOUT THE ILLUSTRATOR

GEORGE ULRICH was born in Morristown, New Jersey, and received his Bachelor of Fine Arts degree from Syracuse University. He has illustrated several books, including *Make Four Million Dollars by Next Thursday!* by Stephen Manes and *The Amazing Adventure of Me, Myself and I* by Jovial Bob Stine. He lives in Marblehead, Massachusetts, with his wife and two sons.